Josie and the Pussycats
Archie
Rockin' the World
D1367908

STORY AND PENCILS BY:
DAN PARENT

INKS BY:
RICH KOSLOWSKI

LETTERING BY:
JACK MORELLI

COLORS BY:
DIGIKORE STUDIOS

CLASSIC STORIES WRITTEN BY:
FRANK DOYLE • GEORGE GLADIR

CLASSIC STORIES ILLUSTRATED BY:
DAN DECARLO • HARRY LUCEY
RUDY LAPICK • BILL YOSHIDA

Publisher/Co-CEO: **Jon Goldwater**
Co-CEO: **Nancy Silberkleit**
President: **Mike Pellerito**
Co-President/Editor-in-Chief: **Victor Gorelick**
Chief Creative Officer: **Roberto Aguirre-Sacasa**
SVP - Sales & Business: **Jim Sokolowski**
SVP - Publishing & Operations: **Harold Buchholz**
SVP - Publicity & Marketing: **Alex Segura**
Executive Director of Editorial: **Paul Kaminski**
Production Manager: **Stephen Oswald**
Project Coordinator: **Joe Morciglio**
Proofreader/Editorial Assistant: **Jamie Lee Rotante**
Book Design: **John J. Hill**

ISBN: 978-1-61988-907-1

WILD WORLD TOUR
THE GLADS
The BINGOS
Josie AND THE PUSSYCATS
THE Archies

CHAPTER ONE

WELCOME TO MUMBAI!
Mumbaī Svāgata!

Location: Mumbai, India
Continent: Asia
Population: over 13 million

Size: 600 square km
Spoken Languages: Marathi, Hindi, English

Mumbai is the wealthiest and most populous city in India, and the fifth most populous city in the world. However, this large and heavily populated city started out in the Stone Age as an archipelago, or cluster, of seven separate islands. Between the 2nd century BCE and the 9th Century BCE, the islands were transformed into a center of Hindu and Buddhist culture and religion.

In the 1500s, the Kingdom of Portugal gained control of the islands, calling them Bombaim, derived from Bom Bahia which means "the Good Bay." The British then gained control of Bombaim in the 17th Century, and the name was anglicized as "Bombay." Under British rule, it became a major trading town and a large-scale civil engineering project merged all seven islands into a single landmass.

During the mid-18th Century, the city became the world's chief cotton-trading market, resulting in a huge economic boom that enhanced the city's stature—which then allowed the city to become a strong base for the Indian independence movement. Economic and educational development characterized the city during the 19th century with the first-ever Indian railway line beginning operations in 1853. In present day, the Mumbai suburban trains are the lifeline of the city, carrying more than 7.2 million commuters every day. The city was renamed "Mumbai" in March, 1996, derived from the name of an ancient Goddess of the Koli fishing community, Mumba Devi and Aiwhich in Marathi means mother.

When Archie & the gang visit Mumbai, Archie meets Amisha Mehta, a popular Bollywood star in Mumbai. Bollywood is the Hindi film industry based in Mumbai, which produces nearly 200 films every year. The name Bollywood is a blend of Bombay and Hollywood. The 2000s saw a growth in Bollywood's popularity overseas. This led filmmaking to new heights in terms of quality, cinematography and innovative story lines as well as technical advances such as special effects and animation. Bollywood is the largest film producer in India and one of the largest centers of film production in the world.

Planning a visit to Mumbai? Be sure to visit the beautiful Sanjay Gandhi National Park, which is a 104-square-kilometer park that lies within a major metropolitan area. This protected forested area houses around 5000 insect species, 1000 plant species, 250 bird species, and 40 mammal, 38 reptile species, and nine amphibian species, including leopards, deer, crocodiles, snakes and monkeys. This amazing park also houses ancient Buddhist caves dating all the way back to the first century! Mumbai is the only city in the world to have a fully functioning national park with freely roaming large carnivores, within city limits.

Archie

THE ARCHIES

JOSIE & THE PUSSYCATS

THE BINGOS

THE MADHOUSE GLADS

BATTLE OF THE BANDS

The Archies ROCKIN' WORLD TOUR PART ONE!
BOLLYWOOD LOVE!
I DID IT!! I'VE ALMOST SOLD MY FIRST DOCUMENTARY PITCH TO A MAJOR HOLLYWOOD STUDIO!
THAT'S GREAT, RAJ!
WHAT'S THE DOCUMENTARY ABOUT?
IT'S ABOUT YOU GUYS! THE ARCHIES!
WHAT?! HOW'D WE GET INVOLVED IN THIS?
1

WELL, I SHOWED HIM ALL OF THE FOOTAGE I SHOT OF The ARCHIES SINCE I MOVED TO RIVERDALE!
THEY WANT TO DO A CONCERT FILM / DOCUMENTARY OF YOUR UPCOMING TOUR!
WITH ME AS THE DIRECTOR!
WELL, ARCHIE! THIS IS OUR FIRST WORLD TOUR! WE KICK IT OFF IN MUMBAI, INDIA!
IT WOULD BE GOOD PROMOTION!
THIS IS TURNING OUT TO BE SOME TOUR!
YEAH! WE'VE GOT The BINGOS AND The MADHOUSE GLADS ON THE BILL, TOO!
WE'LL NEED OUR MANAGER TO WORK OUT THE LOGISTICS!
I'M ON IT!
HI MARCY!
2

SO...
Pinnacle PICTURES
ALL RIGHT! I THINK WE'RE HEADING IN THE RIGHT DIRECTION ON THIS!
WE JUST FEEL THE TOUR IS MISSING ONE THING!
WHAT'S THAT?
JOSIE AND THE PUSSY-CATS!!
BUT THEY'RE HEADLINING THEIR OWN TOUR!
WE FEEL THERE'S A DYNAMIC BETWEEN The ARCHIES AND THE PUSSYCATS THAT IS IMPORTANT!
WE THINK WE NEED THAT TO "CLINCH" THIS DEAL!
AH, YOU MEAN THE ROMANCE BETWEEN ARCHIE AND VALERIE?
YOU COULD SAY THAT!
WHEN WE WATCHED RAJ'S FOOTAGE OF The ARCHIES, ONE THING RIVETED US...

THE DYNAMIC RELATIONSHIP BETWEEN VALERIE AND ARCHIE!
THERE'S ONE PROBLEM! ARCHIE AND VALERIE HAVEN'T SPOKEN IN MONTHS! THEY'RE ON THE OUTS!
WELL, SEE IF YOU CAN INTEREST THE PUSSYCATS IN JOINING YOU! THEN MAYBE SPARKS WILL FLY AGAIN!
SO...
NOW, MARCY...
WHY WOULD JOSIE AND THE PUSSYCATS TOUR WITH The ARCHIES? THEY'RE HEADLINERS!
WHAT IF THE PUSSYCATS AND The ARCHIES SHARED THE BILL?
WELL, WHAT'S IN IT FOR US?
A DOCUMENTARY MADE BY PINNACLE STUDIOS!
PINNACLE?
WOW!
4

THAT WOULD BE A GREAT PROMOTION!
BUT ARCHIE AND VALERIE ARE ON THE OUTS! THEY MAY NOT WANT TO DO IT!
YEAH... WHAT CAN WE DO ABOUT THAT?
MEANWHILE...
Hmm-mm
OH, HELLO, VALERIE!
HELLO, ARCHIE! FUNNY RUNNING INTO YOU HERE.
YEAH, WELL...
I HAVE JUST ONE THING TO SAY TO YOU...
PUCKER UP, RED!!
5

GIGGLE!
THIS IS SORT OF FUN, SNEAKING AROUND!
HEY, IT'S THE ONLY WAY TO KEEP THE PRESS AWAY! THEY ALMOST RUINED US WITH ALL THAT FOLLOWING US AROUND!
BY PRETENDING WE'RE NOT INVOLVED EVERYTHING IS SO MUCH EASIER!
YEAH, AND IT KEEPS BETTY AND VERONICA OFF MY BACK!
C'MON, LET'S GO HANG OUT IN MY GARAGE!
WE CAN WRITE SOME SONGS, TOO!
OR NOT.
6

SOON...
TOUR WITH THE ARCHIES? FOR A DOCU-MENTARY TOO?
SOUNDS LIKE A GREAT OPPORTUNITY!
BUT WITH YOU AND ARCHIE NOT TALKING...
I SAY WE SHOULD DO IT! IT'S A GREAT OPPORTUNITY! ARCHIE AND I SHOULDN'T BE AN ISSUE...
AND...
THE PUSSYCATS HAVE AGREED TO JOIN THE TOUR!
BUT THERE IS THE ISSUE OF YOU AND VALERIE!
I'M A PROFESSIONAL! LET'S DO IT!
GREAT!
SO...
HA! WE GET TO TOUR TOGETHER!
DO YOU THINK WE SHOULD KEEP UP THIS CHARADE?
7

IF WE WANT THE PRESS OUT OF OUR BUSINESS, YES!
OKAY! IF JAY-Z AND BEYONCE HID THEIR ROMANCE FOR SO LONG, SO CAN WE!
SO...
OKAY, BINGOS! ARE YOU READY TO PLAY MUMBAI?
I CAN'T WAIT!
AND MADHOUSE GLADS! ARE YOU READY?
GATE 7
YOU BET!
WHERE ARE THE ARCHIES?
THEY GET THEIR OWN PRIVATE JET! THEY ARE HEAD-LINERS, AFTER ALL!
WOW! MUST BE NICE!
The Archies
AS DO JOSIE AND THE PUSSYCATS!
OF COURSE!
Josie
8

SO...
WOW! IS MUMBAI REALLY INDIA'S BIGGEST CITY?
IT SURE IS!
Hotel Mumba
IT FEELS GOOD TO BE BACK!
IT'S BEEN A WHILE SINCE I'VE BEEN HERE!
OH, LOOK! THE PUSSYCATS ARE HERE TOO!
HELLO, GIRLS!
ER...HELLO, ARCHIE.
HELLO, VALERIE.
Wink!
giggle!
YOU CAN CUT THE TENSION WITH A KNIFE!
9

I KNOW! ISN'T IT GREAT?!
LEAVES ROOM FOR ME AND ARCHIEKINS!
HE'S JUST AS MUCH MY ARCHIEKINS AS HE IS YOURS!
THE PAPARAZZI ARE EATING THIS UP!
WHILE VALERIE AND I WILL GO COMPLETELY UNNOTICED!
SO...
THE BINGOS SOUND GREAT!
The BINGOS
THE MUMBAI COLISEUM IS AMAZING!
NEXT UP ARE THE MADHOUSE GLADS!
AND The ARCHIES WON TONIGHT'S COIN TOSS-- SO THEY CLOSE THE SHOW!

HOORAY!
YAY!
BRAVO!
WOW! THIS IS THE BIGGEST AUDIENCE WE'VE EVER PLAYED FOR!
HEY, GANG! YOU KNOW MR. DRUMMEL!
THE HEAD OF OUR RECORD LABEL!
YOUR NEW CD IS REALLY TAKING OFF!
YOUR NEW SONG, "HOT FOR YOU... (CUZ UR COOL)" IS CHARTING HERE IN INDIA!

THAT'S GREAT!
WE WANT YOU TO SHOOT A VIDEO FOR THE SONG!
EVEN BETTER!
AND YOU HAVE A BIG FAN WHO'S ALSO A BOLLY-WOOD SUPERSTAR!
BOLLY-WOOD?
THAT'S THE TERM THEY USE FOR INDIA'S MOVIE INDUSTRY!
IT'S THE BIGGEST IN THE WORLD NEXT TO AMERICA'S. ANY-WAY, THIS IS AMISHA MEHTA!
SHE'S THE BIGGEST YOUNG STAR IN INDIA!
AND SHE'S A FAN OF YOURS!
SHE'S AGREED TO BE IN THE VIDEO WITH YOU!
WE CAN DO THAT!
ER... WHEN I SAID YOU, I MEANT ARCHIE --THERE'LL BE NO BAND IN THIS VIDEO!
12

THIS IS MORE OF A CONCEPT VIDEO!
WELL, WHO AM I TO ARGUE?
SOON!
HELLO, ARCHIE! I'M HONORED TO MEET YOU!
SAME HERE, AMISHA! YOU'RE BEAUTIFUL!
GAG ME WITH A SPOON!
IT'S SO EXCITING TO FILM THIS VIDEO ON THE STREETS OF MUMBAI WITH YOU!
THERE'S A LOT OF DANCING ON THESE STORY-BOARDS!
I DO A LOT DANCING IN MY FILMS!
LET'S START REHEARSING.
Hmph! WE GET VALERIE OUT OF THE PICTURE, AND NEW COMPETITION MOVES IN!
WE DON'T KNOW THAT! MAYBE SHE'S OKAY!
I DON'T KNOW...
13

LOOK AT THE WAY SHE LOOKS AT HIM!
Hmm! WE BETTER KEEP AN EYE ON THEM!
sigh!
WOW! THEY LIGHT UP THE SCREEN! EVEN DANCING THROUGH ALL THIS RAIN! IT NEVER RAINS LIKE THIS HERE!
I'VE NEVER SEEN ARCHIE DANCE LIKE THAT!
MAYBE YOU DON'T INSPIRE HIS DANCE MOVES!
SPLASH
IT'S STOPPED RAINING! LET'S GET THE CLOSE-UPS IN BEFORE IT RAINS AGAIN!
Hmm... THAT AWNING LOOKS AWFULLY FULL OF WATER...
oh, REGGIE...

I'M ON IT.!
I'M HAPPY TO RAIN ON ARCHIE'S HAPPY PARADE!
Oh, MY LOVE...
YOU'RE SO HOT 'CUZ YOU'RE SO COOL!
DRIP
BLINK
SPLOOSH
MMM!!
SPTOOi!!
JUST KEEP ROLLING!
I LIKE IT.!!
15

I'D LIKE TO KISS YOU!
WE DON'T KISS ON FILM HERE IN INDIA!
JUST LOOK INTO MY EYES.
THAT WORKS, TOO!
THAT'S A WRAP!
Oh, BROTHER! MORE COMPETITION!
AND THE PRESS GOES WILD...
MUMBAI REPORTER
IS IT TRUE LOVE for ARCHIE & AMISHA?!
The PULSE
IT'S Archie & Amisha!!
BOLLYWOOD ROMANCE
LOVE BIRDS HOLDING HANDS?
16

the Archies
THIS IS MAKING FOR ONE EXCITING DOCUMENTARY!
AMISHA IS JOINING ARCHIE ONSTAGE!
THEY'RE GONNA SING TOGETHER!
I'M GONNA DIE!!
I KNOW THIS IS PROBABLY JUST FOR PUBLICITY...
...BUT I HAVE TO FIND OUT IF ARCHIE REALLY LIKES HER!

ARCHIE, DO YOU STILL LOVE ? OR DO YOU HAVE FEELINGS FOR AMISHA?
VALERIE, I LIKE AMISHA...
gulp!
BUT I LOVE YOU!
THAT'S MY RED!
LATER...
I'LL HAVE TONS OF GREAT FOOTAGE FOR THE DOCUMENTARY!
ARCHIE CARRYING ON WITH THIS AMISHA GIRL...
WELL, I DON'T LIKE IT!
wha?!

CHERYL BLOSSOM?! WHAT ARE YOU DOING HERE? WITH ALEXANDRA CABOT OF ALL PEOPLE?!
I'M HERE TO OVERSEE THINGS!
THIS DOCUMENTARY IS GETTING OUT OF CONTROL!
WHAT DOES THIS HAVE TO TO DO WITH YOU?!
HAVEN'T YOU READ THE TRADES?
PINNACLE PICTURES WAS RECENTLY ACQUIRED...
HOLLYWOOD TIMES
...BY NONE OTHER THAN BLOSSOM ENTERPRISES!
BLOSSOM ENTERPRISES ACQUIRES PINNACLE!
WHAT?!
SO YOU BASICALLY WORK FOR ME!
19

SO CHERYL BLOSSOM IS RUNNING THIS SHOW NOW!
WITH THE HELP OF MY NEW BFF-- ALEXANDRA CABOT!
ANY QUESTIONS?
NEXT UP → The TOUR CONTINUES-- IN CHINA!
AND WITH MORE SURPRISES!
SURPRISES LIKE SPECIAL GUEST STAR--
Sabrina
THE TEENAGE WITCH
End

CHAPTER TWO
阿奇
Dan Parent

Location: Shanghai, China
Continent: Asia
Population: 23,470,000
Size: 2448 square miles
Spoken Languages: English, Wu Chinese, Mandarin

WELCOME TO SHANGHAI!
Shang Hai Huan Ying Ni!

Shanghai is the most populous city in China as well as the world. Shanghai grew in importance in the 19th Century, when it flourished as a center of commerce between East and West, and became the undisputed financial hub of the Asia Pacific in the 1930s. It has since been described as the "showpiece" of the booming economy of China. The name "Shanghai" comes from the Chinese characters meaning "above" for Shang and "Sea" for hai, together meaning "Upon the Sea."

Want to know how to navigate Shanghai? It's quite easy—the city has the largest bus system worldwide with over 1400 bus lines! It's a great and affordable way to get around, but if you're looking for speed you may want to check out the Shanghai Magley Train, which is the world's fastest passenger train. It can reach a maximum cruising speed of 267.81 miles (431 kilometers) per hour—wow!

Shanghai has one of the top shopping centers in all of Asia. Veronica will love exploring both the affordable markets of Nanjing Road and the luxurious shopping centers west of Nanjing Road.

When Archie and the gang arrive in Shanghai, you may have noticed a yellow and red tower with spheres. That is the Oriental Pearl TV Tower, located in Pudong Park in Lujiazui, Shanghai. The tower creates a picture of "twin dragons playing with pearls" with radiant three-dimensional lighting. It stands at a whopping 156 feet high—making it China's second tallest TV and radio tower.

Location: Beijing, China

Continent: Asia

Population: 20,693,000

Size: 6487 square miles

Spoken Languages: Mandarin, English

WELCOME TO BEIJING!

Huanying Lai Beijing!

Beijing, sometimes referred to as Peking, is the capital city of China and second largest Chinese city after Shanghai. It is the nation's political, cultural and educational center, as well as a major hub for the national highway, expressway, railway and high-speed rail networks.

While on their trip to Beijing, The Archies have the amazing opportunity to sing in front of the historical Great Wall of China! The Great Wall of China was constructed over about 2000 years by several different Chinese emperors, starting in BC 475. It was built to protect the people from their enemies at the time, the Huns. Rather than being one long continuous wall, the Great Wall of China is actually made up of a number of different sections. It is the longest structure ever built by humans—stretching around 3915 miles (6300 kilometers) in length. If you measure the length of all the different sections of the wall, the length is more like 13670 miles (22000 kilometers).

While The Archies and Josie and the Pussycats put on a rockin' show in Beijing, one of the most important aspects of Chinese culture is music—specifically the Peking (or Beijing) Opera. The Peking Opera is a combination of songs, dialogues, fighting, acrobatics and more.

Speaking of can't-miss sights in Beijing, the Forbidden City—a huge palace built during the Ming Dynasty to the end of the Qing Dynasty—is located in the center of the city.

THE ARCHIES, JOSIE & THE PUSSYCATS, THE BINGOS, THE MADHOUSE GLADS

"Love on the Road"
The ARCHIE'S ROCKIN' WORLD TOUR!
PART 2
BUT HERE'S A RE-CAP OF LAST ISSUE!
THE ARCHIES, THE PUSSYCATS, THE BINGOS, AND THE MAD-HOUSE GLADS HAVE EMBARKED ON A WORLD TOUR STARTING IN INDIA!
IT'S BEING DOCU-MENTED BY RAJ PATEL FOR THE MAJOR STUDIO PINNACLE FILMS!
The Archies
The Archies
ARCHIE AND VALERIE HAVE REKINDLED THEIR ROMANCE (ALBEIT, IN PRIVATE).
BUT ARCHIE HAS BEEN PAIRED WITH BOLLYWOOD SUPERSTAR AMISHA MEHTA--AND THERE'S DEFINITELY A CONNECTION!
AND SUDDENLY, PINNACLE STUDIOS HAS BEEN PURCHASED BY BLOSSOM ENTERPRISES, AS IN CHERYL BLOSSOM!
HOW WILL THIS EFFECT THE DOCUMENTARY? AND THE TOUR? FIND OUT AS THE TOUR ARRIVES IN CHINA!
CHINA
1

I'VE NEVER BEEN TO SHANGHAI!
IT'S CHINA'S BIGGEST CITY!
WE HAVE A CONCERT THERE! BUT WAIT UNTIL WE GET TO BEIJING!
WHAT'S GOING ON THERE?
OUR BIGGEST CONCERT! IN FRONT OF THE GREAT WALL OF CHINA!
WHAT'S SO GREAT ABOUT IT?
ARE YOU KIDDING?
IT'S THE LARGEST FREE STANDING FORMATION IN THE WORLD! IT'S OVER 13,000 MILES LONG!
I'M NOT SO SURE ABOUT THIS!
I THINK THE GOBI DESERT IS A BETTER BACKDROP!

WHY IS SHE HERE?
WITH THAT TROUBLEMAKER ON HER SIDE?
I OWN PINNACLE STUDIOS NOW! SO I OWN THIS DOCUMENTARY!
TREAD CAREFULLY, CHERYL!
THIS DOCUMENTARY CAPTURES EVERYTHING... INCLUDING MANIACAL DIVAS WHO THINK THEY CAN CONTROL EVERYTHING!
BESIDES, I'M UPLOADING LITTLE SNEAK PEEKS DAILY! YOU WOULDN'T WANT TO LOOK BAD, WOULD YOU?
UH, WELL... NO...
AND YOUR DADDY OWNS THE STUDIO! YOU WOULDN'T WANT HIM TO GET MAD AT YOU, WOULD YOU?
ER... UH, WELL...
OKAY! I SEE WHERE YOU'RE GOING...
3

BUT BE CAREFUL! BECAUSE I'M STILL HERE WATCHING WHAT'S GOING ON!
PSSST! CHERYL!
I THOUGHT YOU SAID WE'D BE ABLE TO JOIN THE PUSSYCATS WITH YOUR NEW-FOUND POWER!
WE WILL! WE'LL FIGURE OUT A WAY!
BESIDES, I'LL HAVE PLENTY OF TIME TO PLAN...
I WON'T BE GETTING ANYWHERE WITH ARCHIE... HE'S SO BUSY WITH THAT AMISHA!
WHY IS SHE TRAVELING TO CHINA WITH US?
THE RECORD COMPANY LIKES HER!
Hmmm... WHERE'S THAT MUSIC COMING FROM...?
4

BETTY? ARE YOU PLANNING A SOLO ACT?
LET'S JUST SAY THE TAMBOURINE HAS ITS LIMITS!
OH, AND LOOK! YOU'RE SKYPING WITH GINGER, MIDGE, TONI AND SABRINA!
WE'RE JUST DOING A LITTLE CHICK ROCK 'N' ROLL THING!
COOL! CAN I GET IT ON TAPE?!
NOT QUITE YET! I DON'T THINK WE'RE READY!
WELL, MOST OF YOU ARE READY!
I'M STILL A LITTLE SHAKY ON KEYBOARD!
YOU'RE DOING JUST GREAT, SABRINA!
SABRINA! WHY DON'T YOU USE YOUR MAGIC AND OUTPLAY EVERYONE?
THE FUN PART IS LEARNING! I WANT TO BE A SKILLED MUSICIAN!
5

WELL, GOOD LUCK, BETTY!
:SIGH: IT'S NOT LIKE I HAVE ANY ROMANCE TO KEEP ME BUSY!
I WISH TREV* WAS ON THE PLANE WITH ME!
*TREV IS VALERIE'S BROTHER. BETTY AND TREV DATED BACK IN ARCHIE: A ROCK 'N' ROLL ROMANCE.
SO...
WOW! SHANGHAI IS BEAUTIFUL!
WE'LL BE PLAYING THAT ARENA OVER THERE!
I WISH WE WERE HEAD-LINING!
6

SOMEDAY, SAMANTHA! The ARCHIES ARE SO LUCKY!
I WISH I HAD ARCHIE'S LUCK WITH THE LADIES!
HE AND VALERIE ARE QUITE THE TICKET!
DON'T YOU MEAN WERE THE TICKET? THEY'RE NOT TOGETHER ANY-MORE!
Oh, YES THEY ARE!
WELL, WILL YOU LOOK AT THAT!
THAT REMINDS ME, I SAW SOME INTERESTING FOOTAGE OF ARCHIE AND AMISHA...
SO...
RUN THAT BY ME AGAIN, RAJ...
I WANT TO KISS YOU...
AGAIN...
I WANT TO KISS YOU...
7

SO...
ARE YOU RECORDING?
NO! IF YOU WANT TRASHY REALITY, YOU RECORD IT!
FINE, I WILL! THIS IS REAL STUFF, LIKE IT OR NOT!
OKAY, YOU TWO...
I KNOW ALL ABOUT YOU TWO SNEAKING AROUND!
I'VE GOT IT ON TAPE!!
OKAY! OKAY! SO SUE US!
I THINK IT'S GREAT YOU TWO CAN BE SO DEVOTED!
BUT IT MUST BE TOUGH FOR YOU, VALERIE.
CONSIDERING ARCHIE'S FEELINGS FOR AMISHA!
AMISHA AND ARCHIE ARE ONLY MUSICAL PARTNERS! THAT'S ALL!
8

OH, REALLY? WATCH THIS, VALERIE!
I WANT TO KISS YOU...*
WE DON'T KISS ON FILM HERE...
*SEE LAST CHAPTER!
YOU WANTED TO KISS HER?
THAT LOOKED PRETTY REAL, ARCHIE!
I... I WAS JUST CAUGHT UP IN THE MOMENT!
WHEN WILL I LEARN?
I'M JUST ONE IN YOUR HAREM OF GIRLS THAT YOU GO THROUGH. WELL, YOU CAN REMOVE ME FROM YOUR ROTATION!
VALERIE! PLEASE!!
THANKS A LOT, CHERYL!
9

WHAT DID THAT ACCOMPLISH, CHERYL?
ARE YOU KIDDING?! SOMEONE MIGHT ACTUALLY WATCH THIS DOCUMENTARY NOW!
SO...
OH, ARCHIE! YOU POOR THING! YOU AND VALERIE BELONG TOGETHER!
BUT YOU AND I HAVE TO GO ON SOON!
CHEER UP!
SO...
PUSSYCATS! YOU WERE GREAT!
YEAH!
YOU WERE GREAT, VALERIE!
BREAK YOUR HEAD!
DON'T YOU MEAN LEG?
YOU HEARD ME!!
10

YOU'RE ON!
GO!
ARCHIE'S MIND IS ELSE-WHERE!
I THINK IT'S MORE VALERIE STUFF!
SIGH I REMEMBER WHEN HE USED TO GET WORKED UP OVER US!
SOON!
AND NOW A DUET WITH THE COUPLE OF THE YEAR... ARCHIE & AMISHA!
the Archies
AS MUCH AS I LOVE SINGING WITH ARCHIE...
HE SHOULD BE PERFORMING WITH THE ONE THAT HE REALLY LOVES...

...VALERIE SMITH.!
GET OUT HERE!
The Archies
HUH?
GO ON, VALERIE! THEY'RE CALLING FOR YOU!
UH, ER-- UH--
GO ON.!!
YAY!!!
THAT WAS NICE OF YOU, AMISHA!
WELL, IT'S JUST THAT ARCHIE IS SUCH A NICE GUY!
WE THOUGHT YOU TWO WERE GOING TO BE A COUPLE!
SIGH
SO DID I!
12

OH, BABY, MY WORDS ARE TRUE...
BUT MY HEART IS BLUE
BEAUTIFUL!
I GUESS THEY'RE BACK TOGETHER!
WOO!!
THAT WAS GREAT!
ENCORE!
I LOVE YOU, VALERIE.
VALERIE...?
WE'RE NOT BACK TOGETHER!
AND I WON'T BE COERCED OR PRESSURED BY ONE SONG TO-GETHER!
OKAY, GLADS! YOU'RE ON!

THE NEXT DAY...
WE'RE OFF TO BEIJING! YAY!
WE GUYS WILL MEET UP WITH YOU ON THE NEXT PLANE!
A BLOG WANTS TO DO A FASHION SPREAD ON US GUYS!
OKAY! THE REST OF US WILL SEE YOU THERE!
SO...
THE GREAT WALL OF CHINA!!
THERE AREN'T MANY CONCERT EVENTS ALLOWED HERE!
THIS WILL BE THE OPPORTUNITY OF A LIFETIME!
14

WE SHOULD PROBABLY START PRE-PARING!
ARCHIE'S FLIGHT SHOULD BE ARRIVING SOON!
DON'T COUNT ON IT!
THE AIRPORT IN SHANGHAI IS SHUT DOWN!
WHAT?!
THERE'S A TROPICAL STORM! THE PLACE IS SHUT DOWN!
YOU'LL HAVE TO GO ON WITHOUT HIM!
WE ONLY HAVE 2/5 OF The ARCHIES HERE!
HOW DO WE HEAD-LINE WITH THAT?
THE BETTYS! IT'LL BE YOUR WORLD DEBUT!
WHAT?!
15

ISN'T THAT THE NAME OF YOUR BAND?!
YES! THE BETTYS!
BUT THE GIRLS ARE BACK IN RIVER-DALE!
NO, WE'RE NOT!
WHA--?! H-HOW--?! WHE--?!
I DON'T KNOW HOW WE GOT HERE EITHER!
?!?
I COULDN'T HELP IT!
WHEN I SAW ON ARCHIE'S FACEBOOK PAGE THAT THEY WERE STRANDED...
I HAD TO POP US OVER HERE TO SAVE THE DAY!
WHY DIDN'T YOU JUST USE YOUR MAGIC TO ZAP The ARCHIES HERE?
oh, WELL! I GUESS I DIDN'T THINK OF THAT.
YEAH, RIGHT! YOU JUST WANT THE SPOT-LIGHT!
16

DO YOU FEEL READY TO GO ON?
WOW! OUR ALL-GIRL BAND PLAYING THE GREAT WALL!!
LET'S SHOW THEM THE MEANING OF GIRL POWER!!
TONIGHT! THE WORLD MEETS THE BETTYS!!
HOW EXCITING! LET'S GET ALL OF THIS ON TAPE!

NO PRESSURE, THOUGH! ONLY HALF THE WORLD WILL SEE IT!
GULP

WOW!
I DIDN'T KNOW THAT BETTY COULD ROCK LIKE THAT!
SHE'S GOT A LOT OF PENT UP ENERGY!
I'M KINDA JEALOUS!
AND PROUD!
The Bettys ARE SMOKING HOT!
The Bettys
YOU SEE THEM, ARCH?
YEAH! THEY SOUND GREAT!
THEY'RE GOING TO OUTSHINE The ARCHIES!

WELL, LET'S NOT GO THAT FAR!
MUST BE NICE TO BE PART OF ALL THAT EXCITEMENT!
SHE'S RIGHT!
THIS IS SUCH A MAGICAL MOMENT!
WE SHOULD ALL BE HERE TO ENJOY IT!
JOSIE and the PUSSYCATS
WE SHOULD ALL BE HERE!
WHAT?!
HOW?!
HUH?!
ZAP
HOW DID WE GET HERE?!
19

NEVER MIND! LET'S JUST ENJOY THE MOMENT!
LOOK AT THOSE FIREWORKS!
YEAH-- THERE'S FIRE-WORKS ALL RIGHT!
NEXT: THE TOUR CONTINUES IN-- Australia WITH KATY KEENE AND OTHER GUEST STARS!
?
?

CHAPTER THREE

WELCOME TO AUSTRALIA!
G'DAY MATES!

Location: Sydney, Australia

Continent: Australia

Population: 4.576 million

Size: 4689 square miles

Spoken Languages: English, Dharug, Iyora

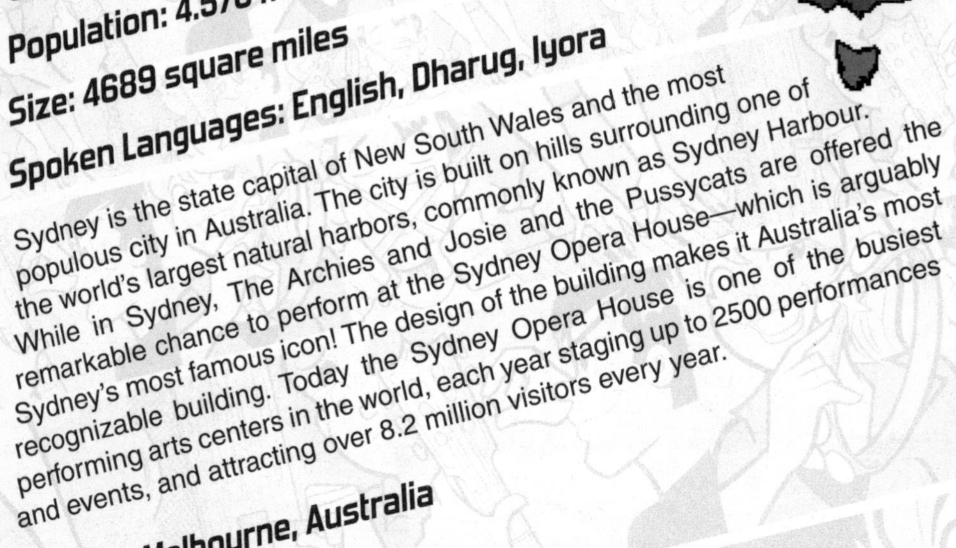

Sydney is the state capital of New South Wales and the most populous city in Australia. The city is built on hills surrounding one of the world's largest natural harbors, commonly known as Sydney Harbour. While in Sydney, The Archies and Josie and the Pussycats are offered the remarkable chance to perform at the Sydney Opera House—which is arguably Sydney's most famous icon! The design of the building makes it Australia's most recognizable building. Today the Sydney Opera House is one of the busiest performing arts centers in the world, each year staging up to 2500 performances and events, and attracting over 8.2 million visitors every year.

Location: Melbourne, Australia

Continent: Australia

Population: 4.077 million

Size: 3400 square miles

Spoken Languages: English

Melbourne is the capital and most populous city in the state of Victoria, the largest city in Australia. It is also the official fox capital of the world—with between six and twenty three foxes per square kilometer in the urban area of the city! If you ever get to Melbourne, check out the historic Luna Park, the world's oldest amusement park. The park houses the world's oldest roller coaster, "The Scenic Railway" as well as a carousel dating all the way back to 1913!

VARIANT COVER #652

LITTLE The Archies®

LIVE IN PERSON

With Josie® & THE PUSSYCATS

And The BINGOS® The Madhouse Glads®

ARCHIE'S ROCKIN' WORLD TOUR PART 3--
BLUNDER DOWN UNDER!
HI! I'M AMISHA! I'M GOING TO GIVE YOU THE RUN-DOWN ON WHAT HAPPENED IN THE LAST ISSUE.!
"The ARCHIES WORLD TOUR CONTINUED INTO CHINA.!
CHINA
"RAJ CONTINUED TO DOCUMENT THE CONCERT-- AS WELL AS ARCHIE AND VALERIE'S BREAK-UP...
R
"...WHICH WAS INSTIGATED BY NONE OTHER THAN CHERYL BLOSSOM AND HER COHORT ALEXANDRA CABOT.!
"WHEN THE BANDS COULDN'T MAKE THEIR CONCERT AT THE GREAT WALL, BETTY'S GIRL BAND, The BETTYS PERFORMED TO GREAT ACCLAIM!"
NOBODY CAN FIGURE OUT HOW THEY GOT THERE... BUT NONE-THELESS, IT WAS A GREAT SUCCESS!
The Betty's
I HAD SOMETHING TO DO WITH IT.!

I CAN'T BELIEVE WE'RE IN SUNNY AUSTRALIA!
SYDNEY IS SO BEAUTIFUL!
I CAN'T BELIEVE WE'RE GOING TO PLAY THE HISTORIC SYDNEY OPERA HOUSE!
YOU'RE GOING TO PLAY IN THE "ROCK 'N' ROLL FASHION-PALOOZA"!
IT'S A BENEFIT, WHERE OUR BANDS WILL PLAY, AS FAMOUS MODELS DISPLAY CLOTHES FOR CHARITY!
DID YOU HEAR THAT, ARCHIE? FASHION MODELS!
2

HE'S STILL BUMMED OUT OVER VALERIE!
C'MON, ARCH!
LIGHTEN UP!
WE'RE IN AUSTRALIA FOR TWO WEEKS!
ENJOY THE SITES OF THIS BEAUTIFUL PLACE!
I WILL!
THERE'S ONE BEAUTIFUL SITE RIGHT NOW!
SO...
I WANNA HOLD YOU 'TIL THE END OF TIME...
OOH! WHAT A BEAUTIFUL SONG!
IT DOES SOUND NICE! AND FAMILIAR!

I KNOW! THAT VOICE DOES SOUND FAMILIAR, DOESN'T IT?
C'MON, ARCHIE! WE'RE OFF TO SEE THE GOLD COAST!
MIND IF I JOIN YOU?
HEY! YOU'RE...
KATY KEENE!
THAT'S RIGHT!
I'M ORGANIZING THE ROCK N' ROLL FASHION PALOOZA!
I THOUGHT WE COULD GO OVER THINGS WHILE SIGHT-SEEING!
SURE THING!
RAJ! SHOULDN'T YOU BE FILMING THIS?
HAHA!
I THINK RAJ IS ENAMORED WITH KATY!
4

SO...
THE GOLD COAST IS BEAUTIFUL!
IT SURE IS!
I'M GLAD ARCHIE CAME!
I THINK HE'S GOTTEN HIS MIND OFF OF YOU-KNOW-WHO!
SIGH!
MEAN-WHILE...
SO THIS IS ROYAL NATIONAL PARK!
ROYAL NATIONAL PARK

LOOK AT ALL OF THE LIPTAUCUS TREES!
ER... THAT'S "EUCALYPTUS" MELODY!
AND LOOK AT THAT KANGAROO! IT HAS A JOEY IN ITS POUCH!

:GASP!:
THERE'S A KID NAMED JOEY IN THAT KANGAROO'S POUCH?!
NO, MELODY! JOEY IS A NAME FOR A BABY KANGAROO!
Oh, LOOK AT THAT KOALA!
HAVE YOU EVER SEEN SUCH AN ADORABLE FACE?
HE IS CUTE!
KINDA REMINDS ME OF SOMEONE...
SO, The BINGOS AND The MADHOUSE GLADS HIT MELBOURNE...
WOW! IT TOOK ONLY THREE HOURS ON THE BULLET TRAIN TO GET TO MELBOURNE...
6

WHY DIDN'T WE HANG AROUND SYDNEY LONGER?
I FEEL LIKE A THIRD WHEEL AROUND THE ARCHIES AND THE PUSSYCATS!
I KNOW! AND WE'RE THE FOURTH WHEEL!
BESIDES, "THE DAMAGED GOODS" ARE ON TOUR, AND I WANT TO SEE THEIR SHOW HERE!
NOW PLAYING!
THE DAMAGED GOODS!
THE SHOW'S BEEN CANCELLED! THE BAND BROKE UP!
ARE YOU SURE?
I SHOULD KNOW! I'M THEIR MANAGER! WANT TO FILL IN FOR THEM?
YOU KNOW WHO WE ARE?!
OF COURSE! YOU'RE MY FAVORITE PART OF THE ROCKIN' WORLD TOUR!
7

REALLY? WOW! NICE TO BE NOTICED!
WE'LL DO IT!
SHOULDN'T WE CHECK IN WITH THE OTHERS?
THIS WON'T INTERFERE WITH OUR TOUR!
BESIDES! IT'S TIME FOR THE BINGOS AND THE GLADS TO TAKE CENTER STAGE!
HERE, HERE!
YOU'RE ON IN TWO HOURS!
AND...
SO KEEP IN MIND, YOU GUYS WILL WALK THE RUNWAY TOO!
WHEN THE OTHER BANDS ARE PLAYING, YOU'LL STRUT YOUR STUFF!
I WANNA HOLD YOU 'TIL THE END OF TIME...
8

THERE'S THAT SONG AGAIN!
Ah, YES! SHE'LL BE PART OF THE FASHION EVENT, TOO!
OF COURSE, YOU ALL GO BACK TOGETHER, DON'T YOU?
??
THAT VOICE! I JUST FIGURED OUT WHO IT IS!
THEN TELL ME!
IT'S OUR OLD PAL...
LATER...
BRIGITTE REILLY!!
YAY! IT'S BEEN SO LONG!!
WE'VE MISSED YOU SINCE YOU GRADUATED EARLY FROM RHS!
WELL, I WANTED TO FOCUS ON MY MUSIC!
9

WE HEAR YOUR SONG EVERY-WHERE!
I KNOW! IT'S A HIT HERE DOWN UNDER!
IT'S GOING TO BE RELEASED IN THE STATES NEXT MONTH!
I'M SO NERVOUS!
SHE'S SO MODEST!
LOOK! SHE'S ON THE COVER OF THIS AUSSIE MAGAZINE!
"BRIGITTE!"
WOW! YOU KNOW YOU'VE MADE IT WHEN YOU GO BY ONE NAME!!
AUSSIE MUSIC
Brigitte
SO, YOU TWO ARE STILL BATTLING IT OUT FOR ARCHIE?
THAT'S COMPLICATED!
IT ALWAYS WAS!
WE'LL FILL YOU IN...
10

THE NEXT DAY...
THE BINGOS AND THE GLADS GOT A GREAT REVIEW AT THEIR SHOW LAST NIGHT!
BINGOS ROCK THE HOUSE
I DIDN'T KNOW THEY WERE PERFORMING!
NEITHER DID I...

SO...
WE'VE BEEN OFFERED THE REST OF "THE DAMAGED GOODS" DATES HERE IN AUSTRALIA!
WE CAN STILL PERFORM ON OUR TOUR! BUT WE REALLY WANT TO DO THIS!

WELL, I SUPPOSE!! JUST TELL US UP FRONT NEXT TIME!
YOU GOT IT!
WE'RE PERFORMING IN TOWN TONIGHT...

WOW! THEY ARE REALLY GOOD!
THEY'VE REALLY HIT THEIR STRIDE!
I'M GLAD WE LET THEM DO THEIR OWN THING!
HI, VALERIE!
HI, ARCHIE!
HEY, KIDS! WHAT'S UP?!
WHAT A PAIN THAT CHERYL IS!
12

AND ALEXANDRA'S NOT MUCH BETTER!
WE'VE GOT TO GET ARCHIE AND VALERIE ALONE TO PATCH THINGS UP!
THINK! THINK! I KNOW!
THERE'S A LITTLE DINGY TOUR RIGHT OUT OF MELBOURNE!
I'VE BEEN CALLED A LITTLE DINGY BEFORE!
WHAT A SHOCK!
ANYWAY, IF WE CAN GET THEM ALONE...
LATER...
GUYS! IT'S TWO DAYS UNTIL THE SHOW!
YOU ALL HAVE TO BE FITTED FOR YOUR OUTFITS!
13

YAY! SOMEONE'S SPEAKING MY LANGUAGE!
THE LANGUAGE OF VAPID!
I HAVE SOMETHING BLACK AND BLUE FOR YOU TO WEAR!
SO...
WOW! YOU ALL LOOK GREAT!!
PUSSYCATS WALK ON THE RUNWAY WITH THE GLADS IN TEN!

BRIGITTE! YOU'RE UP NEXT!
GORGEOUS!
The ARCHIES ARE GOING TO PLAY NOW!
the Archies
WE'RE ALL HERE!
WHERE'S ARCHIE?!
the Archie
I--I CAN'T MOVE! THESE PANTS ARE TOO TIGHT!
THAT'S WHAT HAPPENS WHEN YOU DON'T COME TO THE FITTING!
AND THESE BOOTS ARE TOO HIGH!
NO TIME TO CHANGE! YOU'RE ON!!
OMIGOSH! HE'S WADDLING LIKE A DUCK!
C'MON!

WE'LL CARRY HIM OUT!
MEN ARE SUCH DOLTS SOME-TIMES!
SO...
THAT WAS OKAY! AS LONG AS I DON'T HAVE TO MOVE, I'M FINE!
OKAY, GUYS! HIT THE RUNWAY WHILE THE PUSSYCATS PLAY!
WHAT?! I CAN'T GO ON ANY RUNWAY LIKE THIS!
IN THE NAME OF FASHION, DON'T MESS THIS UP!
ARCHIE! GO!!
OMIGOSH! HE'S HOPPING LIKE AN IDIOT!
THAT'S OUR ARCHIE!
HA! HA! HA!
CLOP CLOP CLOP
16

WELL, HE IS ENTERTAINING THE CROWD!
Whoops!
R-R-R-RIIIP!
YIKES! POOR ARCHIE!!
THEY'LL SEE YOUR UNDER-WEAR!!
B-BUT--
--I'M NOT WEARING ANY! I COULDN'T GET THESE PANTS ON OVER THEM!
HERE, RED!
COVER YOURSELF UP FOR CRYING OUT LOUD!
YOU CALLED ME RED!
DON'T GET ALL MUSHY! I JUST DIDN'T WANT TO SEE YOU HUMILIATED!

AWWW... ISN'T THAT SWEET!
WE HAVE A SPECIAL TREAT!
BRIGITTE WANTS TO PERFORM HER HIT "END OF TIME"!
YAY! WOO-HOO!!
I'M DEDICATING THIS TO ARCHIE AND VALERIE!
I'VE BEEN MISSING YOUR TOUCH...
GREAT! A BALLAD BY BRIGITTE! ARCHIE AND VALERIE ARE AS GOOD AS GOLD!
...I WANNA HOLD YOU 'TIL THE END OF TIME...
WE STILL HAVE TO TALK!
THAT'S GOOD ENOUGH FOR ME!
I WISH I HAD SOME-ONE TO HOLD!
18

HI, BABY!
Oh, COME HERE!
HI, TREVOR!
HI, BETTY!
HELLO, TRIPLE DECKER BURGER!
SO...
AUSTRALIA WAS GRAND!
IT WAS EVEN BETTER SEEING BRIGITTE AGAIN!
WE RAISED SO MUCH MONEY FOR CHARITY!
THANKS TO ALL OF YOU!
HEY, WHERE ARE ARCHIE AND VALERIE?

WELL, WE HAD SET UP A LITTLE DINGY FOR THEM!
ARE YOU TALKING ABOUT MELODY?
THAT JOKE'S BEEN USED, DOLT!
I HOPE THEY'RE TALKING IT OUT!
"I HOPE SO!"
NEXT:
the WORLD TOUR WINDS UP IN CANADA!
End

CHAPTER FOUR
Dan Parent

WELCOME TO CANADA!

A MARI USQUE AD MARE!

Location: Vancouver, British Columbia, Canada

Continent: North America

Population: 578,040

Size: 44.39 square miles

Spoken Languages: French, English, Cantonese, Tagalog, Punjabi

Vancouver is a coastal seaport city on the mainland of British Columbia, Canada. It is one of the most ethnically and linguistically diverse cities in Canada, with 52% of its residents having a first language other than English. The top immigrant language in Vancouver is Punjabi. Punjabi, Cantonese and Mandarin account for 40% of the population of Vancouver that have an immigrant language as a main home language.

The amount of ethnic and cultural diversity is probably why Metro Vancouver has become one of the largest film production centers in North America, earning Vancouver the nickname "Hollywood North." Many films and TV programs set in the United States have actually been filmed in Vancouver!

Location: Calgary, Alberta, Canada

Continent: North America

Population: 988,195

Size: 208.5 square miles

Spoken Languages: French, English

Calgary is the the largest city in Alberta, Canada. It is recognized as a Canadian leader in the oil and gas industry as well as a leader in economic expansion.

Despite being the business and financial center of Canada and boasting the strongest economy in the entire country, Calgary is referred to as "Cowtown" by many and upholds an image of the Wild West because of the Calgary Stampede, an annual 10-day event that bills itself as "The Greatest Outdoor Show on Earth." This event features the world's largest rodeo, concerts, a midway, various exhibits, agricultural competitions, stage shows and a parade.

On their stop in Calgary, the bands play the Scotiabank Saddledome, which is the primary indoor arena of Calgary. The facility hosts concerts, sporting championships and events for the Calgary Exhibition and Stampede.

Location: Toronto, Ontario, Canada

Continent: North America

Population: 2.503 million

Size: 243.2 square miles

Spoken Languages: English

Toronto is the most populous city in Canada and the capital of Ontario, with a population of over 5 million. It is an important destination for immigrants to Canada, and it is one of the world's most diverse cities, with about 49% of the population born outside Canada.

While in Toronto, Archie and the gang take in a view of the CN Tower. The CN Tower is a 1,815.4 ft tall concrete communications and observation tower in Downtown Toronto. It was built in 1976, becoming the world's tallest free-standing structure and world's tallest tower at the time.

The bands play the final show of their tour at the famed Air Canada Centre, home of the Toronto Maple Leafs and the Toronto Raptors.

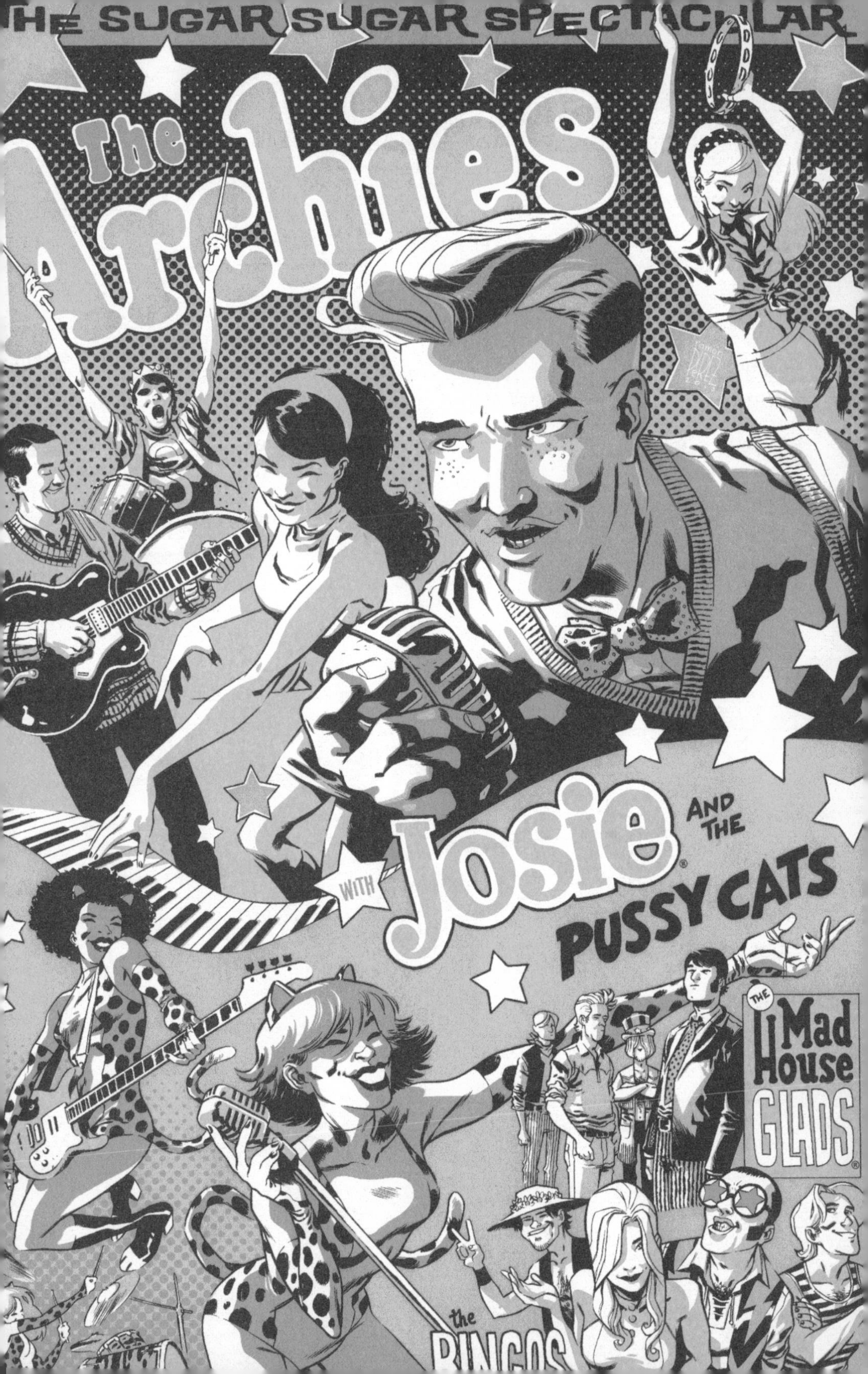

THE SUGAR SUGAR SPECTACULAR
The Archies
WITH
Josie AND THE
PUSSY CATS
THE Mad House GLADS
the
BINGOS

ARCHIE'S ROCKIN' WORLD TOUR
PART 4
"CLOSE TO THE BORDERLINE"
KATY KEENE HERE! GIVING YOU A RE-CAP OF LAST ISSUE!
"THE ARCHIES AND THE OTHER BANDS CAME TO AUSTRALIA FOR THEIR TOUR... AND MY ROCK N' ROLL FASHION SHOW!
AUSTRALIA
"ARCHIE AND VALERIE WERE STILL ON SHAKY GROUND...
"...WHILE THE BINGOS AND THE GLADS HAD BRANCHED OUT ON THEIR OWN!
"OLD FRIEND BRIGITTE REILLY RETURNED!
"AND A NEW FRIEND AMISHA SORT OF WATCHED ON THE SIDELINES. I THINK SHE LIKES A CERTAIN REDHEAD!
"BUT THE BANDS MADE THEIR FANS HAPPY IN AUSTRALIA!
"AND ARCHIE AND VALERIE FOUND PEACE WITH EACH OTHER..."
...AND NOW FOR THE TOUR'S GRAND FINALE IN CANADA!

WE'RE HERE IN VANCOUVER! OUR FIRST STOP!
IT SEEMS WEIRD TO BE HERE WITHOUT THE BINGOS AND THE GLADS!
THEY'LL BE HERE FOR OUR FINAL SHOW IN TORONTO!
THEY'RE HAVING ALL KINDS OF SUCCESS DOWN UNDER IN AUSTRALIA!
WE CAN'T BEGRUDGE THEM THAT!
SURE WE CAN! SNICKER!
YOU HAVE TO GO WHERE THE FANS ARE!
SO TRUE!
WHICH REMINDS ME! IT'LL BE SPLITSVILLE AGAIN FOR US AFTER THIS TOUR!
I KNOW! I KNOW!
2

THE PUSSYCATS SOLO TOUR BEGINS!
AND I HAVE TO GO BACK TO HIGH SCHOOL!
WHY DID I HAVE TO FALL IN LOVE WITH AN OLDER WOMAN?
I'M 3 YEARS OLDER! WHAT'S THE BIG DEAL?
I GUESS THAT MAKES YOU A COUGAR! YOU EVEN HAVE THE COSTUME FOR IT!
GET THIS ON TAPE, RAJ!
MY GOAL IS TO GET SOME HUMILIATING FOOTAGE OF CHERYL!
I CAN DREAM...
3

WOW! VANCOUVER HAS ALL KINDS OF FILMING GOING ON!
VANCOUVER IS OTHERWISE KNOWN AS HOLLYWOOD NORTH!
BECAUSE OF ITS ECONOMICAL ADVANTAGE, MANY SHOWS AND MOVIES FILM HERE!
I LOVE IT! IT'S SO PEACEFUL...
WHAT DO YOU MEAN...
IN INDIA I'M A HUGE STAR! I GET FOLLOWED EVERYWHERE!
BUT HERE, I'M BARELY RECOGNIZED!
OH, I'M SORRY.
OH, DON'T GET ME WRONG! I LOVE IT!
YOU DO?
IT FEELS GOOD TO BE WITH PEOPLE MY AGE! TO HANG OUT... AND BE NORMAL!
4

WOW! IF YOU THINK *WE'RE* NORMAL, YOU NEED *HELP*!
YOU'RE ALWAYS WELCOME TO HANG WITH US ANYTIME!
THANK YOU!
I HATE TO BREAK THIS UP, BUT WE HAVE A *SHOW* IN AN *HOUR*!
SO...
WE'RE REALLY ROCKIN' *ROGERS ARENA*!
AND ARCHIE AND AMISHA SOUND AS SWEET AS EVER!
the Archies

AFTER THE SHOW...
TIME TO GET SOME *SHUT EYE*!
WE'RE OFF TO *CALGARY* TOMORROW!
WHY SO *SAD*, AMISHA?

Oh, I'M NOT SAD! I'M HAPPY!
HAPPY THAT I GOT TO MEET YOU ALL!
MY NEW FRIENDS! I HOPE WE STAY THIS WAY!
OF COURSE, AMISHA!
WE'RE ALWAYS YOUR FRIENDS! THAT'S THE RIVERDALE WAY!
I SENSE AMISHA DOESN'T HAVE A LOT OF FRIENDS BACK HOME!
SHE'S BEEN A STAR SINCE SHE WAS A LITTLE GIRL!
SHE DOESN'T HAVE WHAT ALL OF YOU HAVE...
...A NORMAL TEEN-AGE LIFE!
WOW! YOU KNOW, WE REALLY TAKE THINGS FOR GRANTED SOME-TIMES!
6

SOMETIMES JUST HAVING FRIENDS WHO CARE ABOUT YOU IS EVERY-THING!
FWAP
AND SOMETIMES WE'RE STUCK WITH BUFFOONS WHO NEED TO BE TAKEN DOWN! PREPARE TO DIE, DOOFUS!
HA!
HA!
HA!
HA! HA!

CALGARY!
WOW! IT LOOKS LIKE THE WILD WEST OUT HERE!
CALGARY IS HOME TO THE CALGARY STAMPEDE!
AND JUST LOOK AT THOSE ROCKY MOUNTAINS!

WE PLAY THE SADDLEDOME TONIGHT!
BUT LET'S GET IN SOME SIGHT-SEEING FIRST!
THAT NIGHT...
THERE'S BEEN A CHANGE IN PLANS!
AMISHA HAD TO HEAD BACK TO INDIA...
I KNOW! I JUST GOT A TEXT!
HAVE SOME THINGS TO TAKE CARE OF... BUT I'LL SEE YOU ALL SOON! I HOPE! -AMISHA
POOR GIRL! I HOPE SHE'S OKAY!
WELL, WE CAN'T WORRY ABOUT THAT NOW!
WE NEED A REPLACEMENT FOR ARCHIE AND AMISHA'S DUET!
8

NO TIME TO FLY IN BRIGITTE OR ANYONE ELSE!
IT'LL HAVE TO BE SOMEONE HERE!
I HAVE A SUGGESTION!
WHAT A SURPRISE!
SO!
THIS IS IT! OUR TIME TO SHINE!
YOU'RE GOING TO DO THE DUET WITH ARCHIE!
REALLY? HOW?!
WHEN VALERIE GOES TO CHANGE INTO HER OUTFIT FOR THE DUET--
--I'LL SEE THAT SHE STAYS PUT!
THE YOU RUN OUT AND SAVE THE DAY.!!
PLUS, IT'LL GIVE THIS BORING DOCUMENTARY THE KICK IN THE PANTS THAT IT NEEDS!

FINALLY! I'LL BE A STAR! GRAMMY AWARDS, WATCH OUT!
UH... TAKE IT DOWN A NOTCH, ALEXANDRIA!
THAT NIGHT!
YOU'RE UP NEXT, VALERIE!
OKAY! GOTTA CHANGE FROM PUSSY-CAT...
...TO SEXY CHANTEUSE!
NOW, I'VE GOT TO...
HEY! THE DOOR IS LOCKED!
I'D BETTER CALL FOR HELP...
I'LL TAKE THAT!
CHERYL! WHAT ARE YOU UP TO NOW?!
IT'S TIME FOR YOU TO TAKE A BACK SEAT, SISTER!
WHO'S GONNA MAKE ME?!
10

SHOVE
GET IN THIS CLOSET!!
WE'RE STAYING IN HERE UNTIL ARCHIE AND ALEX'S MUSICAL NUMBER IS OVER!
ALEXANDRA?! SHE CAN'T SING! SHE'LL MAKE A MOCKERY OF THE WHOLE SHOW!!
HA! WE AUTO-TUNED AND PRE-RECORDED HER PART FOR HER TO LIPSYNC! AND WE KNOW THAT AUTO-TUNE CAN MAKE A HOWLING COYOTE SOUND GOOD...!
SO...
WHERE IS SHE?! ARCHIE'S SWEATING BULLETS!!
HE NEEDS HELP UP THERE!
POOR GUY!
I'M HERE TO...
I'LL HELP OUT!!

OMIGOSH! IT'S CANADIAN SUPERSTAR CELINE DIJON!
WHAT A COINCIDENCE THAT YOU HAPPEN TO BE HERE!
I'M A HUGE FAN! MAY I?
YOU BETCHA!
AND YOUR LOVE IS SO REAL...
IT SOUNDS GREAT FROM HERE!
THAT DOESN'T SOUND LIKE ALEXANDRA!
WAH!
CHERYL! OPEN UP!!
WHAT'S GOING ON?!
WHAT HAPPENED?!
I WAS PUSHED ASIDE BY NONE OTHER THAN CELINE DIJON!!
12

WHAT?! CAN'T YOU DO ANYTHING RIGHT?!!
HONESTLY! AM I THE ONLY ONE WITH A BRAIN HERE?!
YOU BOOBS! ONLY YOU TWO COULD IMPROVE THE CONCERT BY ACCIDENT!
WOW! THEY SOUND GREAT!!
A STANDING OVATION!
WAY TO GO, CHERYL!
IT WAS AN HONOR TO SING WITH YOU!
VALERIE! WHAT HAPPENED?
IT'S A LONG STORY!
BUT A GOOD ONE!
:SNICKER!:
NEXT STOP, MONTREAL!
OH, HOW I LOVE THIS CULTURAL OLD CITY!
13

IT'S OLD ARCHITECTURE IS SO BEAUTIFUL! ESPECIALLY IN THE "OLD MONTREAL" SECTION!
BONJOUR! COMMENT CA VA AUJOURD'HUI?
AND THE FACT THAT FRENCH IS SPOKEN HERE PRIMARILY IS SO SEXY!
I LIKE THE POUTAIN!
THAT NIGHT AT THE BELL CENTRE...
ARCHIE AND VALERIE! YOU WERE GREAT!
WELL, I'M NO CELINE DIJON, BUT...
Hmm... WHAT'S WRONG?
I JUST REALIZED...
...WE ONLY HAVE ONE CONCERT LEFT... IN TORONTO...
YEAH...
14

THEN IT'S BACK TO SCHOOL...
AND BACK ON THE ROAD...
LET'S NOT GET TOO DEPRESSED! WE HAVE TO GIVE IT OUR BEST YET!
IN TORONTO!
NOTHING LIKE BEING IN CANADA'S BIGGEST CITY!
THERE'S NO VIEW OF TORONTO LIKE THE ONE FROM THE CN TOWER!
YOU CAN SAY THAT AGAIN!
The BINGOS! AND The GLADS!
WE'RE HERE FOR THE GRAND FINALE!
IT WOULDN'T BE THE SAME WITHOUT YOU GUYS!

TELL US ABOUT YOUR OWN TOUR!
WE WOULDN'T HAVE BEEN NOTICED IF IT WASN'T FOR THIS TOUR!
HOW CAN WE EVER THANK YOU?
HOW ABOUT PUTTING ON A GREAT SHOW TONIGHT!
DEAL!!
THAT NIGHT, AT THE AIR CANADA CENTRE!
AND THAT ENDS OUR ROCKIN' WORLD TOUR!
THANKS TO EVERYONE FOR SUPPORTING US!
AND THERE'S JUST ONE THING LEFT FOR US TO DO FOR ALL OF YOU--
16

GROUP JAM!!
SUGAR SUGAR
AWW HONEY HONEY!
Josie and the PUSSY CATS
HOORAY!
YOU ROCK!
YAY!
GO BABY!
WOW! THAT'S IT! I'M SAD!
I'M RELIEVED!
I NEED A NAP!
MY WORK BEGINS NOW! I HAVE HUNDREDS OF HOURS OF FOOTAGE TO POUR THROUGH FOR THE DOCUMENTARY!
17

YOU'LL DO IT AGAIN! THIS IS JUST THE BEGINNING...
SABRINA! HOW DID YOU GET HERE?
YOU ALWAYS SHOW UP UNEXPECTEDLY!
YEAH, HOW ABOUT THAT?
BACK IN RIVER-DALE...
WELL, RED! HERE WE ARE AGAIN!
I HAVE TO HIT THE ROAD...
AND YOU HAVE TO HIT THE BOOKS!
SIGH! HOW DEPRESSING!
YOU'RE IN GOOD HANDS! YOU'VE GOT THE GANG!
YEAH...
WE'LL BE TOGETHER SOON!
VALERIE...
18

...DON'T FALL IN LOVE WITH ANYONE ELSE!
I COULD SAY THE SAME TO YOU!
WE'RE YOUNG! WE HAVE TO REALIZE THINGS CAN HAPPEN...
...BUT AT THE SAME TIME...
...NOBODY COMPARES TO YOU!
I LOVE YOU, VALERIE!
I REALLY, REALLY LOVE YOU!
YOU SOUND SURPRISED!
I THINK I AM!
SMOOCH!
19

EPILOGUE:
ARCHIE!!
WE HAVE A NEW STUDENT HERE AT RIVERDALE HIGH!
NONE OTHER THAN...
AMISHA MEHTA!!
WHAT?! THAT'S AWESOME! BUT HOW? WHAT ABOUT INDIA? YOUR CAREER?
YOU ALL MADE ME REALIZE THE IMPORTANCE OF FRIENDSHIP!
AND THAT I WANT A NORMAL TEEN-AGE LIFE FOR AWHILE!
I CAN'T HAVE ANONYMITY IN INDIA... BUT I CAN HERE!

I FEEL SO WELCOME HERE ALREADY!
THAT'S WHAT HAPPENS HERE IN RIVERDALE! EVERYBODY'S WELCOME HERE!

WELCOME TO RIVERDALE, AMISHA!
END

Josie
AND THE PUSSYCATS
First to take the stage are that pioneering all-girl band, Josie & the Pussycats! The band that inspired a gazillion other girl groups was founded by its lead singer, songwriter and guitarist, Josie. With backup from bombastic bassist Valerie and dynamic drummer Melody, the power trio conquered not just the pop charts, but also appeared in a hit animated TV series and feature-length live-action movie! Josie and the band's debut performance was in JOSIE & THE PUSSYCATS #45 (December, 1969).
Josie
AND THE PUSSYCATS

THE Archies®

Next up are Riverdale's finest, The Archies! Archie and his friends have been rocking for decades, and while their instruments have often been interchangeable, the core of the group remains Archie, Betty, Jughead, Veronica and Reggie. Best-known for their top-selling hit "Sugar, Sugar" The Archies have also rocked Saturday morning TV with one hit cartoon after another! Archie and his band mates strummed their first chords in LIFE WITH ARCHIE #60 (April, 1967) and appeared in many popular comic stories including "Music Soothes" from ARCHIE #185 (Sept., 1968).

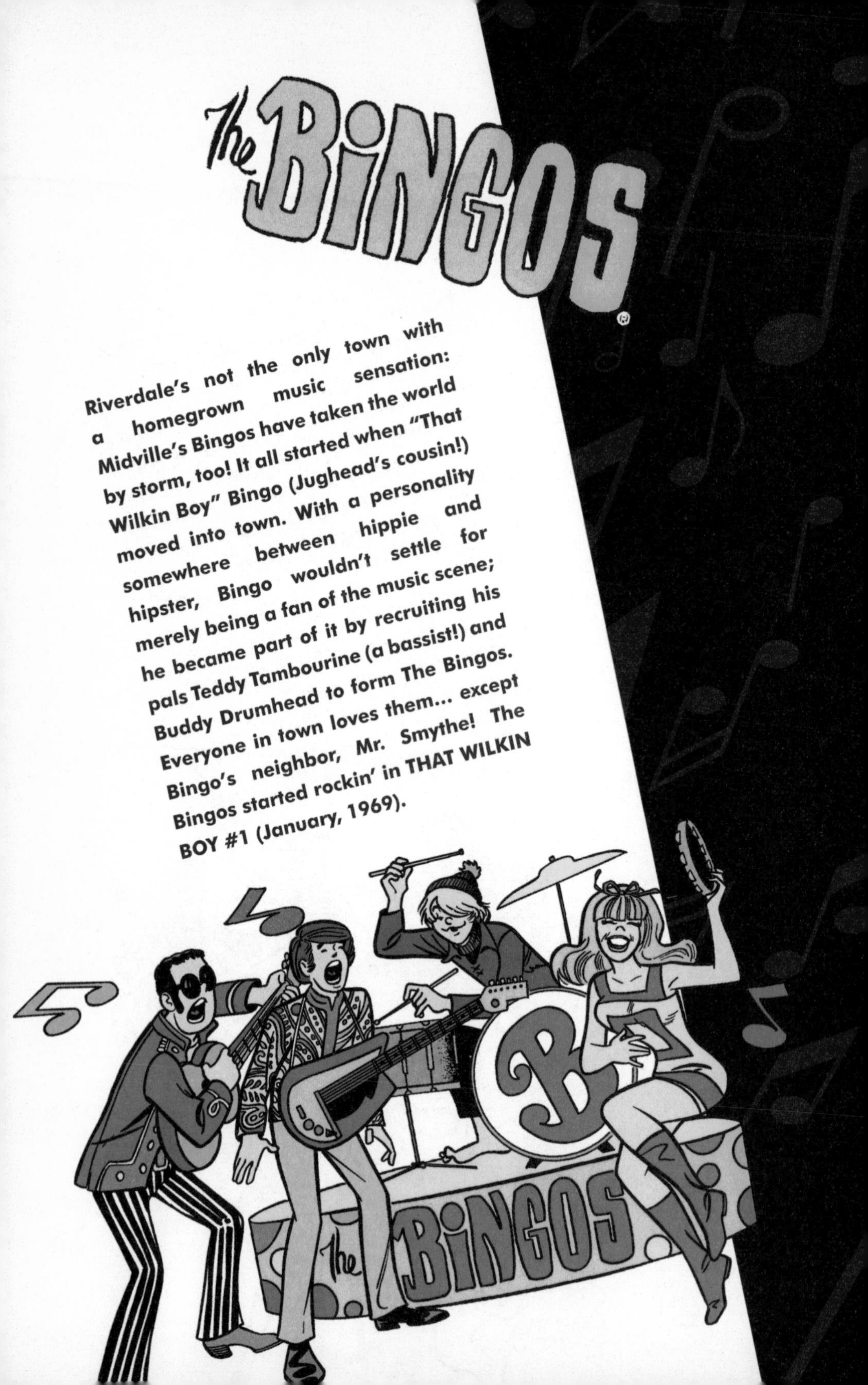
The BiNGOS®
Riverdale's not the only town with a homegrown music sensation: Midville's Bingos have taken the world by storm, too! It all started when "That Wilkin Boy" Bingo (Jughead's cousin!) moved into town. With a personality somewhere between hippie and hipster, Bingo wouldn't settle for merely being a fan of the music scene; he became part of it by recruiting his pals Teddy Tambourine (a bassist!) and Buddy Drumhead to form The Bingos. Everyone in town loves them... except Bingo's neighbor, Mr. Smythe! The Bingos started rockin' in THAT WILKIN BOY #1 (January, 1969).
The BiNGOS

DONUT
GURUS
I
HAVE
KNOWN

The MA-ADS™

The final group in our Rockomixpalooza Fest are the irrepressible Madhouse Ma-Ads! The brainchild of former folk singer Clyde Didit, The Ma-Ads take their inspiration from everything from the 1960s "mod" scene to The Monkees. Like other famous groups such as The Ramones and Traveling Wilburys, each member of the Ma-Ads goes by the same last name – "Didit!" Only they "didit" first! Clyde, Dippy, Dick and Danny Diditmade their first splash on the cover of MADHOUSE MA-AD JOKES #67 (February, April, 1969) followed by a full Ma-Ads story in issue #68. Starting with issue #73, The Ma-ads faced some stiff competition from the Madhouse Glads – so much so that Dippy and Danny Didit ultimately joined the rival band!

Archie

Rockin' the World

BONUS TRACKS

THE Archies in Music SOOTHES
BAYBEH, KISS ME HARD 'N' FAST, HOL' ME TIGHT AN' MAKE IT LAST, LOVE IS ALL AN' ALL IS LOVE, IT TURNS A HAWK INTO A DOVE
IT'S NOT THAT I DON'T LOVE THESE OLD CLASSICS, BUT MY TEETH ARE BEGINNING TO RATTLE!
AND I JUST PUT A CAKE IN THE OVEN!
1

THIS IS SNEAKY, BUT IT'S BETTER THAN HURTING THEIR FEELINGS!
FUSE BOX

HEY! THE AMPS HAVE GONE DEAD!
WE HAVE NO JUICE!
The Archies

BLOWN FUSE, BOYS! ...AND I DON'T HAVE A SPARE!
I'LL BE BACK WITH A NEW ONE IN AN HOUR OR SO!

AN HOUR WILL COOL THE CREATIVE SPARK!
OH?
SORRY, POP! ...WE CAN'T WAIT!

A FINE GROUP OF BOYS! ...AND EXCELLENT MUSICIANS! .... I THINK!
WHY DO THEY ALWAYS PLAY, ..."MUSIC TO BREAK EARDRUMS BY?"

HALT! I APPRECIATE MUSIC AS MUCH AS THE NEXT MAN!
POP'S
CHOCKLIT
SHOP

...BUT THAT STUFF YOU GAVE OUT LAST TIME CURDLED MY CREAM!

WE'RE LIVING IN A CULTURAL DESERT!
ALL CREATIVITY STIFLED BY THE ESTAB-LISHMENT!
YOU'RE MOVING ME TO TEARS!

BUT YOU'RE NOT MOVING INSIDE MY SHOP WITH THOSE NOISEMAKERS!
HEY! WHY DON'T WE PLAY OUT HERE?

ARE YOU NUTS? WHO CAN MAKE MUSIC WITHOUT ELECTRICITY?
I FORGOT!
NO PROBLEM!

I HAVE A LONG EXTENSION CORD!
YOU MEAN WE CAN PLUG IN ON YOUR JUICE?

YOU'RE ALL HEART, POPS!
THAT'S KIND OF YOU, ARCHIE! ACTUALLY, THOUGH, I'M ALMOST ALL FLAB!

OKAY! NOW HIT IT! A-ONE, A-TWO...
The Archies

WHAT A LOVELY FEELING!...TO BE ABLE TO TURN DOWN THE VOLUME JUST BY CLOSING THE DOOR!
OOOH! IT'S THE STREET WHERE WE MEET AND LAY ON THAT BEAT.. IT'S THE SIDEWALK SERENA-ADE

WHIRR!
WHAT THE...?

ZOOM!

THANKS, POPS!...BUT THIS IS TOO DANGEROUS!
POP'S
CHOCKLIT
SHOP

WHY DON'T YOU PRACTICE AT MY HOUSE?
BETTY!...YOU ARE A TRUE PATRON OF THE ARTS!

ISN'T IT GROOVY, MOM? THE ARCHIES ARE GOING TO PLAY RIGHT HERE! ...IN OUR HOUSE!
URK!

IT'S, LIKE, TOO MUCH! EEEE! I CAN BARELY STAND IT!
FUNNY! ALMOST THE VERY WORDS I WOULD HAVE USED!

POPPER DOPPER TEENY BOPPER EENY MEENY MINEY MO! PHONEY BONEY, MACARONI. GO, MAN, GO!
EEP!
5

ER... ARCHIE!... THERE'S JUST NO MEETING OF THE MINDS WITH THE OLDER GENERATION!
I'M AFRAID MOM'S ABOUT TO LOWER THE BOOM!

HAVING LOVE IN OUR HEARTS DOESN'T MEAN NO SMARTS IN OUR HEADS, BETS!
LEAVE THIS TO THE ARCHIES!

OH, SHE'S KINDLY AND GENTLE, SHE'S JUST SUPER DUPER!... IF YOU HAD HER YOU'D WANT FOR NO OTHER! THE BEST OF THE BEST IS OUR OWN, MRS. COOPER, THE EXQUISITE MODEL OF MOTHER!
The Archies

WHAT? I CAN'T HEAR YOU ABOVE THAT DIN!
I SAID, AREN'T THEY GROOVY? ...JUST TOO MUCH! I COULD LISTEN TO THEM ALL NIGHT!
THE END
6

THAT WILKIN BOY IN "SEE SAW"
AN' THEY TOOK HIS HEART AN' STOMPED IT AN' KICKED IT AN' BROKE IT, AN' LITTLE MELVIN MICKLEDINGER CHANGED HIS NAME TO BARRY!
ISN'T THAT A SAD SONG?
THAT GOES BEYOND SAD... ALL THE WAY TO MISERABLE!
RUMP A DUM DUM!
BAP!
BINGO, WHY DON'T YOU AND THE BOYS GO SERENADE OUR NEIGHBOR MR. BIG SHOT SMYTHE, (WITH A "Y", YET!)
CHEE THAT'S GENEROUS OF YOU, DAD! AND ALL THE TIME I THOUGHT YOU DIDN'T LIKE MR. SMYTHE!
DUM DEE DUM DUM! DUM DUM

SAMANTHA SMYTHE, LET'S MAKE THE SCENE, HERE COMES TEDDY TAMBOURINE!

SAM, GET YOUR DEFENSES READY, HERE COMES KNUCKLE-HEADED TEDDY!

BUDDY! PLEASE! NOT ON REBELS HEAD!
PING
THUD
OOH! I OUGHTA GIVE HIM SUCH A NIP!

UH, OH!
WHAT IS IT, DADDY?

IT'S ANOTHER SNEAK ATTACK BY THAT WILKINS!
R·N·G!

WILKIN! NO "S"! JUST PLAIN WILKIN YOU MUSCLE MINDED MORON.!!

MAN! THAT'S WHAT I CALL SENSITIVE!
CLIK!

HERE WE COME, ALL GAY AND JOLLY TO SEE SAMANTHA SMYTHE, BY GOLLY!
DUM THUMP DUM
GOOD GRIEF!

HI, MR. SMYTHE! HI, SAMANTHA!
WELL, IF IT ISN'T THE BINGOS!
HI, BOYS!
SAM GET HIM OFF MY HIGHLY POLISHED MAHOGANY!
RAT-A-TAT-TAT!
PING

KNOCK IT OFF, BUDDY! YOU'RE BUGGIN' THE ESTABLISHMENT!
WAP!

HEY! WHERE DID SAMANTHA AND BINGO GO TO ?
HYUK!

BOY WHAT DOES SHE SEE IN THAT GUY?
OUT OF MY WAY, DOG!
"DOG?" WHAT DOG?

YECH!

ZOUND AND CURSES, AND OTHER UTTERS OF FRUSTRATIONS!!
CHEE! GET HIM!

WHAT I'M GONNA DO IS... I'M GONNA DO SOMETHING DASTARDLY!
I'VE GOT TO WARN BINGO!

I'LL JUST BET THAT GUY'S GONNA DO SOMETHING DASTARDLY!

NOTHING LIKE A COLD SHOWER TO COOL THE BLOOD!

YIKES!
SOMEBODY TURNED ON THE SPRINKLER!
I KNEW HE'D DO SOMETHING DASTARDLY!
SPRITZZ!
SCREECH!

I'LL TURN IT OFF!

?

HMPH! A LITTLE TEDDY BEAR! SOME LITTLE KID MUST HAVE BEEN PLAYING AROUND HERE!

BINGO, BABY! WHEN ARE YOU GONNA GET WISE TO THE TRADEMARK OF TEDDY TAMBOURINE? HOW CAN YOU BE SO DENSE!

I'LL HAVE TO GO HOME AND CHANGE, SAMANTHA! SOME KIDS TURNED ON THE SPRINKLER!
I'LL HAVE TO CHANGE, TOO!

MISSION ACCOMPLISHED, BUDDY! LET'S GO!
RATATATATATAT
POW
KLAK
CRAK
CLIK
TAT
TAT

HA! THAT BINGO'S A DING-A-LING! HE NEVER GETS WISE TO MY LITTLE...
RATATATATATAT
RAT-TAT-TAT
TAT-TATA
TAT-TAT!
TAT TAT!
CREAK

GAK!
CRASH!
KRAK

CAREFUL, REBEL! DON'T HURT YOURSELF WITH THAT SAW!
NOW WHY IN THE WORLD WOULD THAT FOUR LEGGED NUT TAKE MY SAW??
?
!
?
THE End

FRAN the FAN Meets the MADHOUSE MA·ADS

THEY'RE ALL BUSY DOING THEIR THING.!
THE MA-ADS
DO NOT DISTURB
DOWN With
GURUS I HAVE KNOWN

YES, I RECALL READING ZEN WAS CLYDE'S SCENE.!
TRANSCENDENTAL MEDITATION

HMMM.! MAYBE IF I HUM A FEW TIBETAN CHANTS I'LL GET HIS ATTENTION.!
TIBET OR NOT TIBET

OH-MAH.! O-MAH.! OH-MAH.!
?

TSK.! TSK.! POOR GIRL.! SHE MUST HAVE WIGGED OUT AFTER OUR LAST ACT.!
OH-MAH.! OH-MAH.!

HERE! TAKE THIS NOTE TO THE CORNER DRUGGIST! HE'LL KNOW WHAT TO GIVE YOU!

DARN!
Dear Mr. Brown:
THE BEARER IS SUFFERING FROM FAN-ITIS. GIVE HER THE USUAL.
Rx
Clyde Didit

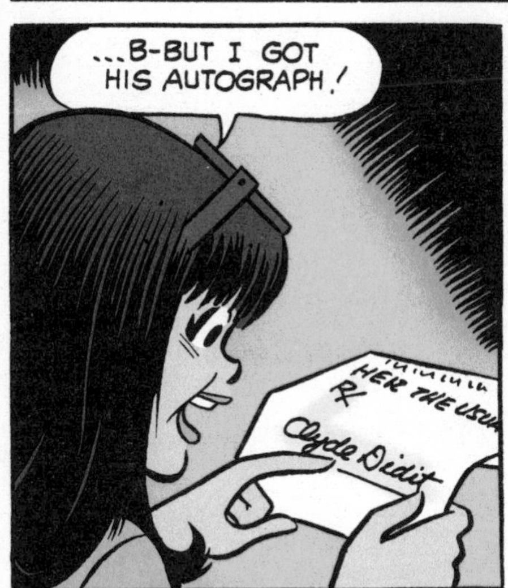
...B-BUT I GOT HIS AUTOGRAPH!
HER THE USUAL
Rx
Clyde Didit

NOW APPEARI
TWO DOWN AND TWO TO GO!
OUR ACT NEEDS A NEW GIMMICK!
DIPPY DIDIT
DICK DIDIT
CLYDE DIDIT
DAN DIDIT

DICK DIDIT, COULD YOU PLEASE...
GO AWAY, GIRL! I HAVE TO THINK!
I BELONG TO Dick Didit

WHY AM I THE ONLY ONE IN THE GROUP WHO WORRIES ABOUT OUR ACT?
OOPS!
CRUNCH!

(GULP!) I'M SORRY I RUINED YOUR GUITAR!
THAT'S IT!! THAT'S OUR NEW GIMMICK!
Dick Didit

AFTER EACH PERFORMANCE WE'LL SMASH OUR INSTRUMENTS!
SMASH
!?

WOW! I'LL HAVE TO TELL OUR MANAGER ABOUT IT!
CAN I HAVE YOUR AUTOGRAPH?

SOME OTHER TIME!
ZIP!
Dick Didit

THREE DOWN AND ONE TO GO!
Dick Didit

DAN, WHERE'S DIPPY?
LOOK FOR THE NEAREST PROTEST DEMONSTRATION! HE'LL BE THERE!!
DONUT
4

THERE HE IS!

DIPPY, CAN I HAVE YOUR AUTOGRAPH?
I'LL GIVE YOU SOMETHING BETTER!
ADMIT TRAN-SYLVANIA TO THE UN

THIS SIGN!!
!?
ADMIT TRAN-SYLVANIA TO THE UN

...NOW I CAN GET TO THE NITTY GRITTY OF MY PROTEST BAG... GRAFFITI!!
?
WHAT ABOUT SENIOR DELINQUENTS?
WHY TRY HARDER?
CONGRESS DECLA
THE N.Y. METS A
DISASTER AREA!
FIGHT AIR POLLUTION! DON'T BREATHE!
EVERYTHING IN AL'S PIZZA JOINT IS CHEEZY!!

THERE! THAT DOES IT!
BUT ALL I WANT IS YOUR AUTOGRAPH!!

SORRY! I'M LATE FOR A 3 P.M. SIT-IN!
SHUCKS!

DECLARES
METS A
ER AREA
ABOVE GRAFFITI
BY Dippy Didit

E'S
A
EA
ABOVE GRAFFITI
BY Dippy Didit

FOUR OUT OF FOUR!
Dippy Didit
FIGHT
AIR POLLU
DON'T
BREATHE!
GRAFFITI

FRAN DID THE IMPOSSIBLE, GANG! SHE GOT ALL OF THE MA-ADS!
GROOVY ROCKERS FAN CLUB
GR
WHERE THERE'S A WILL THERE'S A WAY!
Dippy Didit
Best Wishes Dan Didit
Dear Mr. Brown
Clyde Didit
Dick Didit

AS A TRIBUTE TO HER I'M GOING TO CHANGE THE MOTTO OF YOUR CLUB!

HOW'S THAT?
GR
FRAN
WHERE THERE'S A WILL
THERE'S A WAY
The END

Josie and the Pussycats -in- "DECISIONS DECISIONS"

WHY DO YOU ALWAYS HAVE TO BE A SPOIL SPORT, ALEXANDRA?
SAY WHAT YOU WISH ... I'LL GIVE YOU A LITTLE TIME TO THINK ABOUT IT GIRLS!
CATS

OH SHUCKS, WHAT ARE WE GOING TO DO NOW?

I GUESS WE'LL JUST HAVE TO FORGET THE WHOLE IDEA!

YOU'RE RIGHT, WE CAN'T HAVE A GROUP WITH JUST TWO PEOPLE!

PSST!
?

I COULDN'T HELP BUT OVERHEAR YOUR PROBLEM, GIRLS! HOW WOULD YOU LIKE ALEXANDER CABOT THE THIRD TO HELP YOU OUT?

YOU WANT TO BE A PUSSYCAT? YOU CAN'T EVEN PLAY AN INSTRUMENT!

NOT ME DOLL, ... BUT I KNOW SOMEBODY WHO WOULD BE PERFECT FOR YOUR GROUP!

WHO?
NONE OTHER THAN VALERIE SMITH!

WHO'S VALERIE SMITH?
SHE'S A NEW GIRL IN SCHOOL!

I HEARD HER MAKING WITH THE VOCAL CORDS IN THE SCHOOL AUDITORIUM! SHE'S GOT A VOICE THAT WILL MAKE YOU BLOW YOUR MIND!
WELL, DON'T JUST STAND THERE! GO GET HER!

HANG IN THERE GIRLS! ALEX YOUR NEW MANAGER WILL BE BACK IN A FLASH!

YAHOO! THIS IS MY GOLDEN OPPORTUNITY TO GET IN SOLID WITH JOSIE!

WELL GIRLS! HAVE YOU DECIDED TO SEE THINGS MY WAY?

NO! ALEX IS GOING TO GET US A REPLACEMENT FOR YOU!
WHAT?
4

THAT'S IMPOSSIBLE! WHO CAN HE POSSIBLY FIND THAT COULD BE AS GREAT AS ME?

HERE SHE IS GIRLS! I WANT YOU TO MEET VALERIE SMITH!
HI!

HELLO!
YOU PLAY THE GUITAR, TOO?

SURE!
THAT'S JUST GREAT! LET'S PLAY A LITTLE NUMBER TOGETHER!

AND SO...
WE ARE THE PUSSYCATS WITH A BRAND NEW SOUND IT MAKES YOUR EARS PERK UP AND YOUR HEAD SPIN AROUND!
WHY THAT FINKY BROTHER OF MINE! I'LL FIX HIM!
The PUSSYCATS

ISN'T SHE EVERYTHING I SAID, GIRLS?
WELCOME TO THE GROUP, VALERIE!

DON'T I DESERVE A NICE BIG KISS FOR FINDING HER, JOSIE?
YOU SURE DO, ALEX!

MY BROTHER MAKES ME SO MAD I SEE RED... SO MAKE THAT BRANCH FALL ON HIS *HEAD*!

TOCK!

WHEN YOU GIRLS DECIDE TO CHANGE THE NAME OF THE GROUP GIVE ME A RING!
WOW! WHAT A *KISSER*!!!
YOU'LL GET USED TO IT, VAL! STRANGE THINGS ALWAYS SEEM TO HAPPEN WHEN SHE'S AROUND!
The End